SOCKEYE'S JOURNEY HOME
The Story of a Pacific Salmon

SMITHSONIAN OCEANIC COLLECTION

To Billy, who brought me closer to the salmon—B.W.

To Nicolle, Ryan, and Andrew with love from Aunt J.—J.P.

Illustrations copyright © 2000 Joanie Popeo.
Book copyright © 2007 Soundprints, a division of Trudy Corporation, 353 Main Avenue, Norwalk, CT 06851 and the Smithsonian Institution, Washington, DC 20560.

Published by Soundprints, an imprint of Trudy Corporation, Norwalk, Connecticut.

Art Director: Diane Hinze Kanzler
Book layout: Scott Findlay
Editor: Judy Gitenstein

First Paperback Edition 2007
10 9 8 7 6 5 4 3 2 1
Printed in China

Acknowledgments:
    Our thanks to Dr. Stanley H. Weitzman of the National Museum of Natural History's Department of Vertebrate Zoology for his curatorial review.
    The illustrator would like to acknowledge Dr. C. Bau Taylor and Diane Hinze Kanzler for their assistance.

ISBN-10: 1-56899-755-1 (pbk)
ISBN-13: 978-1-56899-755-3 (pbk)

The Library of Congress Cataloging-in-Publication Data below applies only to the hardcover edition of this book.

Library of Congress Cataloging-in-Publication Data

Winkelman, Barbara Gaines

Sockeye's journey home: the story of a Pacific salmon / written by Barbara Gaines Winkelman; illustrated by Joanie Popeo.—1st ed.
        p.   cm.
"Smithsonian oceanic collection."
Summary: Swimming against the current and avoiding fishing nets and predators, Sockeye Salmon travels from the Pacific Ocean through the Puget Sound, the Ballard Locks Canal, Lake Union, Lake Washington, and up the Cedar River to return to his birthplace and spawn.
    ISBN 1-56899-829-5 (hc.)—ISBN 1-56899-830-9 (micro hc)
1. Sockeye salmon—Juvenile fiction. [1. Sockeye salmon—Fiction. 2. Salmon—Fiction. 3. Animals—Migration—Fiction.] I. Popeo, Joanie, ill. II.Title.
      PZ10.3.W6847 So 2000
      [E]-dc21   99-044598

SOCKEYE'S JOURNEY HOME
The Story of a Pacific Salmon

by Barbara Gaines Winkelman   Illustrated by Joanie Popeo

Soundprints
Where Children Discover...

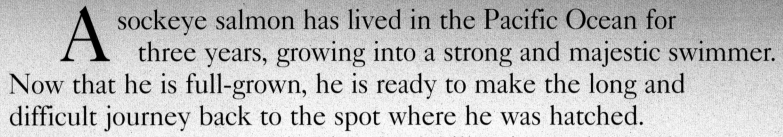

A sockeye salmon has lived in the Pacific Ocean for three years, growing into a strong and majestic swimmer. Now that he is full-grown, he is ready to make the long and difficult journey back to the spot where he was hatched.

Sockeye and others in his school will swim to the northwest corner of Washington State, where the Pacific Ocean meets the Strait of Juan de Fuca. Then they will leave the saltwater behind and enter into the freshwater of Lake Union, Lake Washington, and finally the Cedar River. The Cedar River is the place where Sockeye's life cycle began.

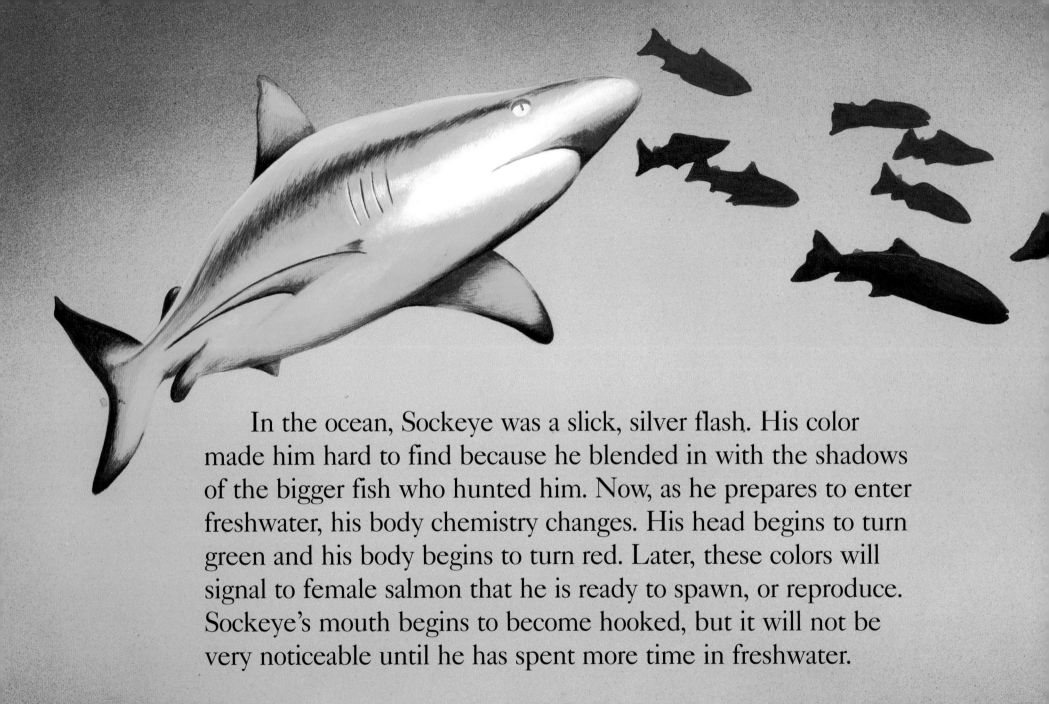

In the ocean, Sockeye was a slick, silver flash. His color made him hard to find because he blended in with the shadows of the bigger fish who hunted him. Now, as he prepares to enter freshwater, his body chemistry changes. His head begins to turn green and his body begins to turn red. Later, these colors will signal to female salmon that he is ready to spawn, or reproduce. Sockeye's mouth begins to become hooked, but it will not be very noticeable until he has spent more time in freshwater.

Sockeye swims east and then south through the Strait of Juan de Fuca, which will lead him to the calmer waters of the Puget Sound. He smells the algae, insects, fish and dust from the rocks of his birthplace three hundred miles away. The scent leads the way, like a compass.

It is midsummer. The air is hot and still. Every year at this time, dangerous predators can be found along the Strait of Juan de Fuca and the Puget Sound. Bald eagles, bears, herds of orca whales, sea lions and harbor seals wait to pounce on the salmon.

A brown black bear dips its paw into the water and scoops up salmon one at at time as they swim by. Sockeye narrowly escapes the bear's claws, but some of the other salmon are not as lucky.

Close by, another bear dips his giant paw and mouth into the water so that he can grab his meal with his sharp teeth. Sockeye escapes the bear's claws with just a gash in his skin.

Sockeye and his school crowd together and continue forward. So strong is Sockeye's instinct to reach his birthing stream that his instinct to eat has been shut off. His body has stored food from his prey in the ocean, making the layer under his skin thick and oily. Now he needs to use this stored energy to swim against the current.

Farther on, there is more danger. Ospreys drop to the water to grab salmon with their claws. Sockeye turns and darts away.

Up ahead Sockeye sees a shadow. The shadow is coming from a boat on the surface of the water. Nearby he sees other fish caught in a net. Sockeye glides around the net to avoid the obstacle.

Sockeye's body continues to change in preparation for spawning. The hook shape of his upper snout is more noticeable. At the same time, his body is adjusting to the gradual changes in the water. The saltwater from the Puget Sound mixes with the canal freshwater leading to Lake Union. This gradual decrease of salt allows Sockeye to adapt to the freshwater that he will inhabit for the remainder of his journey.

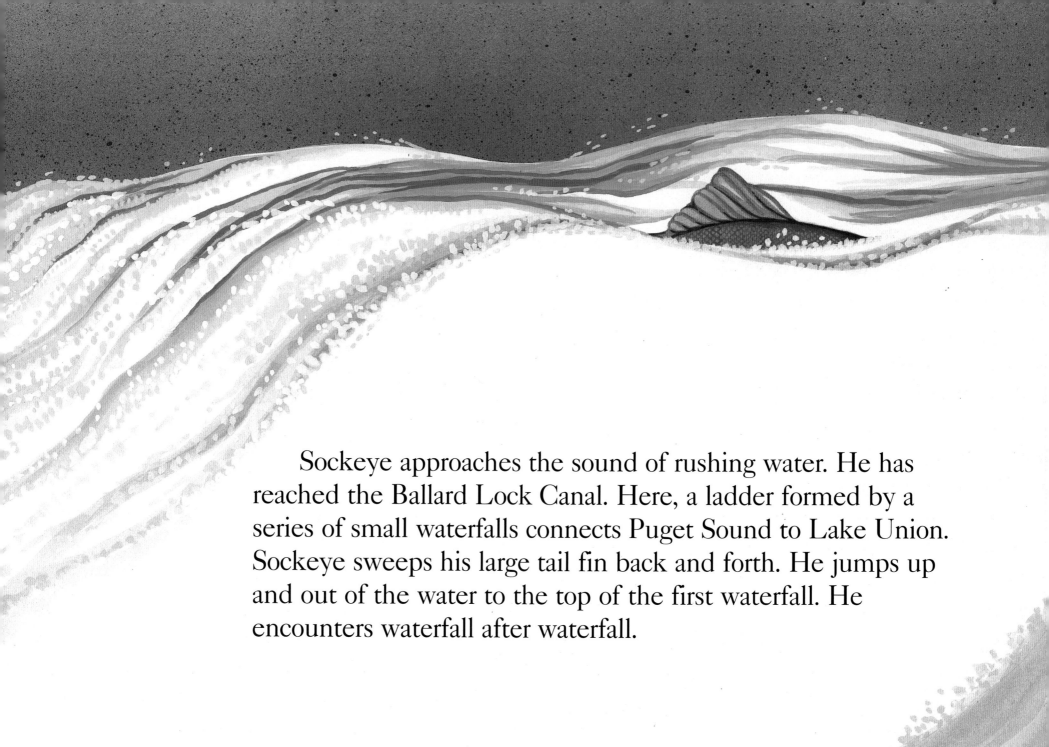

Sockeye approaches the sound of rushing water. He has reached the Ballard Lock Canal. Here, a ladder formed by a series of small waterfalls connects Puget Sound to Lake Union. Sockeye sweeps his large tail fin back and forth. He jumps up and out of the water to the top of the first waterfall. He encounters waterfall after waterfall.

After he has cleared the final waterfall, Sockeye enters Lake Union. He swims across Lake Union and into Lake Washington. Summer has turned to fall when Sockeye reaches the mouth of the Cedar River, the river in which he was hatched.

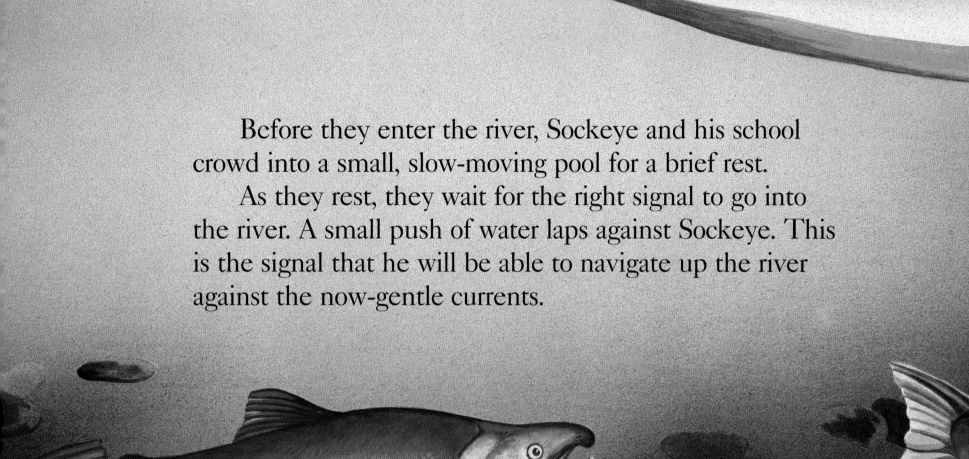

Before they enter the river, Sockeye and his school crowd into a small, slow-moving pool for a brief rest.

As they rest, they wait for the right signal to go into the river. A small push of water laps against Sockeye. This is the signal that he will be able to navigate up the river against the now-gentle currents.

Parts of the river are shallow, and do not cover the salmon. Still, the fish wriggle forward as their exposed backs form a red bridge across the river.

The salmon hear the loud, familiar screeches of seagulls. Several seagulls close in on their prey. The salmon thrash back and forth in warning so the seagulls don't get too close. The seagulls fly away for now. They will wait until the salmon have finished spawning, when they are too weak to resist attack.

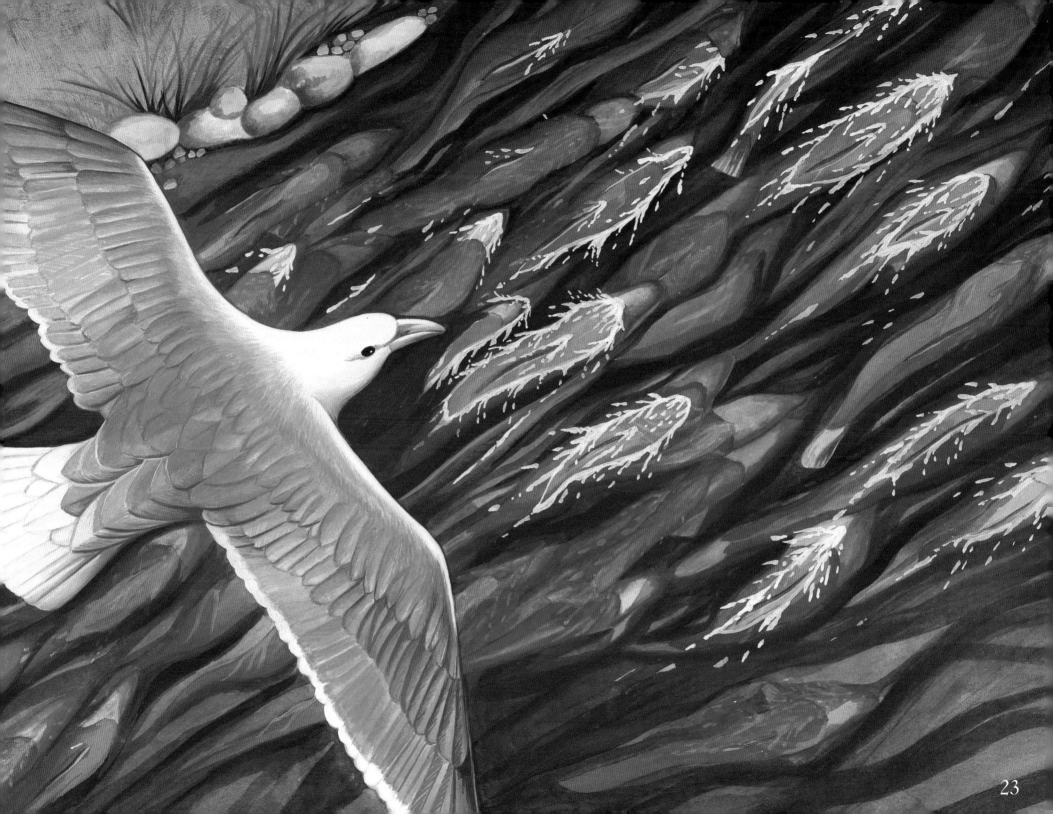

Sockeye has used up a lot of food stored in his body during his trip upstream. As a result, his bright skin fades. His body changes even more in preparation for spawning. As he swims upriver, a hump in his back forms and his teeth grow, protruding from both jaws. He is now ready to fight other males for a female.

Other salmon are pairing as Sockeye arrives at the place where he was hatched. Sockeye swims up to a female and another male that are close by. The female has a pointed snout, which is much different from the male's hooked snout.

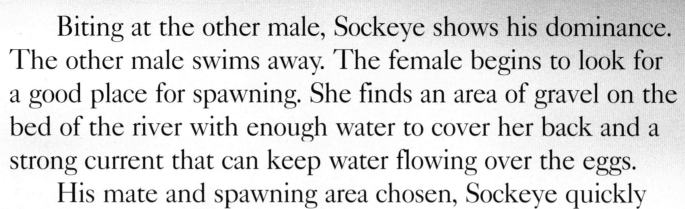

Biting at the other male, Sockeye shows his dominance. The other male swims away. The female begins to look for a good place for spawning. She finds an area of gravel on the bed of the river with enough water to cover her back and a strong current that can keep water flowing over the eggs.

His mate and spawning area chosen, Sockeye quickly gets to work.

Sockeye guards above the spawning area, while the female rolls onto her side, arches her body, and sweeps the gravel and pebbles with her tail fin. She clears a shallow hole. This will be the first nest. When the nest is complete, the female salmon lays amber eggs and Sockeye fertilizes them.

The female salmon moves upstream of this first nest. She sweeps pebbles onto the eggs so that they are protected. Next, the pair goes to another spot close by, where the female will build another nest. The female and male salmon continue to mate with different partners for a few days.

After spawning Sockeye has no energy left. The stored food is used up and Sockeye's body has become thin. Swimming weakly over the redd—the spawning area—he waits for his final rest. His life will end in the area where it started.

In about three months, the eggs will hatch and new salmon fry will go from the Cedar River into one of the freshwater lakes. There they will grow for a couple of years. They will then go out into the Pacific Ocean to grow for another few years. Then they will return to complete their life cycle in this very same river.

About the Sockeye Salmon

The sockeye salmon is one of seven species of Pacific salmon. The sockeye young live up to two years in freshwater, and then up to an additional three years in the Pacific Ocean before returning to the water in which they were hatched. From the ocean to the spawning site, they swim as much as thirty miles a day at three to four miles per hour. On the journey home, sockeye age the equivalent of twenty to forty human years.

Pacific salmon can be found along the Pacific Coast of the United States from California to Alaska and inland to Idaho. They have become extinct among certain parts of Idaho, Montana, Washington and Alaska. In other areas they are endangered. Sockeye salmon have been listed as endangered in the Snake River. Sockeye salmon also live in the western Pacific off the shores of Japan.

Human construction and development are the major causes for a decrease in sockeye population in the past century. Salmon need fresh, clear, cool water to live and spawn. These conditions are changed when a forest is cleared. Mud and sediment due to erosion from deforestation also kill the eggs. Without the trees providing shade over the water, the water is too warm for the salmon to survive.

Attempts to improve the sockeye population are being made by heavily regulating the sport-fishing industry, restoring salmon runs, hatching salmon in captivity, and building cement ladders or throughways next to manmade structures such as dams and canals.

Glossary

current: The part of the water that flows in a certain direction.

fry: Very young and newly hatched salmon. When they get their fins and begin to look like small fish, they are called "juveniles."

headwaters: The origin of a body of water.

life cycle: A predictable pattern from birth to death. A Pacific salmon's life cycle begins and ends in the freshwater in which it was born. In between, the salmon migrates to and from the Pacific Ocean.

mouth: The entrance of a river into another body of water such as a lake, larger river or ocean.

upstream: Moving against the current, toward the headwaters of a stream.

Points of Interest in this Book

pp. 8-9: sea lions, pod of orcas, bald eagle, harbor seals.

pp. 12-13: ospreys.

pp. 22-23: seagull.